Like Father, Like Slaughter

A final girls featurette

Tylor Paige

Copyright © 2024 by Tylor Paige

All rights reserved.

No part of this book may be reproduced in any form or by any electronic or mechanical means, including information storage and retrieval systems, without written permission from the author, except for the use of brief quotations in a book review.

Cover created by Eve Graphic Designs

Edited by Blue Couch Edits

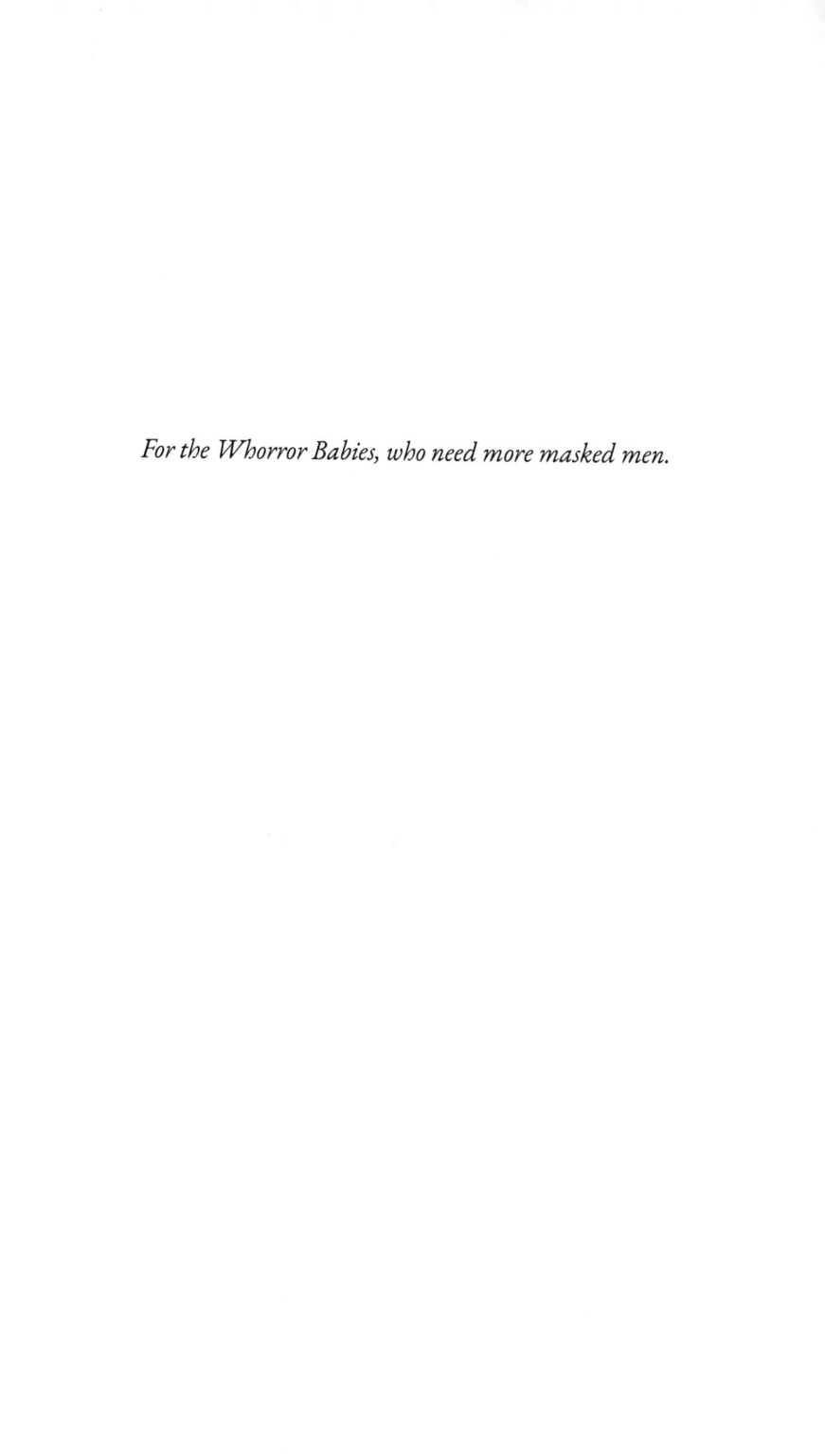

For the Whorror Babies, who need more masked men.

This book is also dedicated to Nick. Thank you, for everything.

Foreword

Hey! So, first off, I hope you enjoy Like Father Like Slaughter. Please consider leaving an honest review wherever you do reviews when you're finished. If you do, tell us what rule was your favorite. I'm partial to Rule 11 myself...

Now, to cover some bases.

Spoiler alerts!

This book is *meant* to be fast paced, absurd, and well, a huge nod to dystopian horror. Not just with the men in masks. That was purely for the Whorror Babies. No, I'm talking about it all. The classic, over the top jerk boyfriend, the creepy aesthetic, the weird secondary plot that kind of just comes in and comes right back out, the quick kills and cheap thrills, and how we move fast to avoid thinking about how stuff doesn't make sense. (Why don't they fight back?) No, this was meant to be fun, spicy, and overall, a short, fun, horror romance novella. Keep that in mind while reading, and I think you'll enjoy the book for what it is. And, as this is just a novella, tell me in the reviews if you like it! If this novella gets popular enough, I'll turn it into a full-length story.

This book is rated R

Like Father Like Slaughter is a horror romance novella with topics that can be upsetting, uncomfortable, and for some, triggering. I encourage you to consider this list to know exactly what you are going to see while reading this book. This story features the apocalypse, spanking, excessive force, abuse of power, purity culture, murder, dub con, brainwashing, gaslighting, people in masks, somnophilia.

Rule One - Eleanor
Celebrate when you can.

"Happy birthday, Eleanor," I said with a bright smile, straightening my posture as I looked at myself in the mirror. "Why, thank you, Milton. I'm glad you came to my party. Is that a present you have there?" I pinched my cheeks to give them some color and glanced down at the counter, picking up the lipstick I had saved from my last exploration above. Should I wear it to my party?

Yes.

I was officially a Young Lady, according to the rules here below. That was my title now that I was an adult. While there were still many things I wasn't allowed to do, I was given permission to wear makeup now. I applied the bright red shade to my lips and grinned. Milton was going to just die when he saw me. I hurried to put on my dress and get going. Glancing at the clock on my bedside table, I realized that the party would start soon, which meant I could make a perfect entrance. I hoped Milton would be waiting for me there with all of our friends.

My heart raced as if I'd just seen a creepie all the way from the Young Ladies' floor to the recreation floor, four stories down. I rode the elevator in silence, even though I wasn't alone. I was never alone.

"Happy birthday, Eleanor."

I looked up at my protector, my guard, my D.A.D.D.Y.

"Thank you, Daddy," I said softly and looked back down at the floor. Daddy was strict and hadn't been enthused when I told him my friends were throwing me a party to celebrate my eighteenth birthday. This was a huge thing for us. I was an adult, but he didn't agree. To him, it was just another day.

"I have a gift for you."

"You do?" I blinked in surprise. My Daddy had only once given me a gift, and it certainly wasn't for a birthday.

"Do you remember when I was assigned to you, ten years ago today, Eleanor?" I nodded, and he continued, "Well, I wanted to celebrate that. It's been a very interesting ten years, wouldn't you say?" He chuckled. Daddy often joked that I had turned his hair gray from the stress of taking me to the world above so often. I was one of the best at finding things, which meant I got to go frequently. But it came at a cost. I had much less free time than my friends.

"Interesting is one word to describe it. Though it hasn't been fun." I pouted as we left the elevator and started down the cold, metal hallway toward the recreation hall.

"Did you expect things to be fun? We have a responsibility to mankind. We don't have time for fun," Daddy recited the speech he'd given me many times over, and I waved his words away.

"Not today, Daddy. Please, just let me have this one night. Let that be your present to me. One night without you watching over me."

His expression darkened. His forehead creased and his eyes turned serious. "That's my job."

"I know but take a day off. It's just a party. Go wherever all the other Daddies in your group go and let me have this one night."

"This is a boy-girl party, isn't it?"

I blushed furiously. "Daddy!"

"You know that Daddies-in-training aren't allowed to date the Young Ladies."

I rolled my eyes. Yes, everyone knew we were untouchable, even to DITs. I was reminded almost daily of the oath we all took so long ago. We reached the doors to the hall, where I could hear music, chatter, and laughter from the other side. I pushed him away gently, and he stepped back.

"Please, Daddy. One night. I just want to dance and eat cake and have punch with my friends. Tomorrow morning, I'll be ready to focus on saving mankind." I saluted him.

He rolled his gray eyes and finally relented.

"Fine. As there are no doubt Daddies-In-Training in there," he nodded to the door. "I know they'll keep you safe, even if you aren't assigned to them. Go, have fun, and I'll see you in the morning, bright and early."

I threw my arms around him. "Oh, thank you, Daddy!" I kissed his cheek and hurried inside, completely forgetting my troubles as my heart soared with joy.

"Happy birthday!" The entire room stopped and turned to me, shouting excitedly. I beamed and hurried over to my best friends, who waved wildly.

"This is amazing!" I gushed, taking in the decor. Pink and gold balloons hung from the ceiling like raindrops of different sizes. Streamers lined the tables and walls, and Frankie Valli played from the radio. "I love this song!"

"I know," Pearl said, grinning. "We've had it on loop since the party started so you could enter to it."

"Oh!" I hugged my beautiful friend with hair the color of the dried grass in the above world — so yellow and bright.

"Your dress is gorgeous. Where did you get that color?"

Olive, our palest friend, tugged on my white skirt. She wore a soft blue dress that matched her blue eyes.

"You like it?" I twirled around. "It was in my CIO box." *Cherished Items Only.*

My friends gasped. Most of our boxes contained photos of people long gone, or records, or books, but hardly ever did one contain clothing.

"Was it a wedding dress?" Olive continued to scrutinize the dress.

"Probably." I shrugged. "I was able to refurbish it into something stylish." I twirled again, and everyone but Olive complimented me. We then hurried to get punch and sandwiches and waited for the boys on the other side of the room to ask us to dance.

After eating, I sat politely with my legs crossed, tapping my foot nervously. Milton wasn't here. He'd promised he'd come. We'd been writing secret notes to each other for months now, and now that I was a Young Lady...

"Happy birthday, Eleanor."

My heart skipped a beat as I turned toward the voice. My smile fell when I saw it was Harold, not Milton.

"Thank you, Harold."

He handed me a present, and I opened it in front of him. "They are leather gloves specifically for the above world. There are plants with sharp leaves that will cut you if you touch them barehanded. Now, you can pick them."

I forced a smile. "This is a wonderful gift."

Dion's song, "Take Good Care of My Baby" came on, and my chin quivered. Was this some weird sign from the universe? Had he ditched me in favor of someone more attainable? We both knew we had to keep our feelings a secret, but he had made me think he liked me just as much as I liked him.

I asked Harold if he had seen Milton.

He perked up and looked around the table at my friends.

"Yeah, he took Cal to get everything ready for, you know"—he leaned in to whisper—"the real party."

"The real party?" I shook my head in confusion. I looked around the table. My friends were grinning deviously.

"It's a tradition," Veronica, my friend with the darkest skin, brightest dress, and smile, said softly, "You don't get to know until it's your time."

I was the youngest out of my group of Young Ladies, and they never stopped reminding me. I crossed my arms like a child.

"Well, now I'm glad Daddy didn't come."

"Eleanor, didn't you notice no one else's Daddy is here?" Helen, the redhead, motioned around the room. I blinked in surprise when I didn't see a single Daddy in sight. She squeezed my shoulders. "It's a rite of passage. You didn't convince him of anything. He's letting you go with us."

"Go where?" Something about this didn't feel right. My nerves were on edge.

Pearl cleared her throat and smoothed her lavender dress. "Will you keep your voice down? We're going to the above world." She said it in a way that made it sound like a secret, but we'd all been there countless times.

"Tonight? Alone?"

Our Daddies would never allow us to go above in the dark, let alone without them.

Olive stood and lightly shoved me. "No, dummy, we'll have the DITs. It's just us, having fun for once."

My stomach churned. I'd never gone up alone before.

Not without my Daddy.

Rule Two - Eleanor
Everything is a risk in the above.

"Should I change?" I asked after we cleaned up the party and were leaving the rec room. "Or will we be seen if we go back?"

"Well, normally, we don't," Veronica said, giving me a side-eye. "Young Ladies don't need to wear PARA Suits, so we can go right on up. However, you are wearing white..."

"It's gonna get dirty." Olive smirked. "And not in the good way."

"You don't know that." Helen giggled. "She *was* looking for Milton."

My cheeks turned hot and I looked at my high heels. I'd spent so much money on them for today. Almost six months' worth of CAFE bucks would be down the drain if I went to the above world in them. On the other hand, if I was caught back in my room by someone not in on the secret, I'd be forced to stay. I couldn't miss my own party.

"I don't have to change. I'll just wash my dress when we get back. No one will know."

With that, we took the stairs to the bunker doors. Pearl flicked on the harsh overhead lights, and we flinched as it stung our eyes. I shivered. No matter how often I came up here, I hated this rust-colored, dirt-smelling, water-dripping room.

The Daddys-In-Training, or DITs, who had attended my formal birthday party were already pulling on their PARA Suits.

Protect against radiation above.

That was the big difference between us and the Daddies. Young Ladies could go up with no protection and be fine. No radiation poisoning, no disgusting rashes, no side effects at all. That's what made us so important.

"You ready?" Norman reached for his gas mask and looked to his fellow DITs. They all slid their masks on and nodded. Norman then turned to us. "Milton and Cal are already above. They've made sure our perimeter is safe, and we are free to enjoy ourselves. Do I have to go through protocol?"

He looked so proud to be the one running us through the rules of going to the above world. The DITs had been training just as long as we had, but they still had three more years to go before officially being assigned to their own Young Lady.

"Yes, Daddy," we said in unison. He scowled at our sarcasm but stood up straight and rattled off the dos and don'ts of going above.

"Do stay within fifteen feet of a Daddy at any given time. Do keep in communication constantly with your Daddy. Our PARA suits are specially made so that you can hear us clearly. Don't touch a creepie. Always be on the lookout for crawlies, and do exactly as your Daddy tells you when you are out of the bunker. Our job is to keep you safe and to bring you back to the bunker. We will do whatever it takes to make that happen. Understand?"

"Yes, Daddy," we said. Norman shoved his mask on and pushed buttons on the wall, opening the vault. As the panel lit up and the door began to squeal in protest of it opening, my heart raced. I couldn't wait to find Milton. If we were able to find a house with a sealed basement, perhaps he could take his mask off for just a bit and we could finally kiss.

The DITs lined up, and when the door opened fully, we walked beside them, taking the ladder up. The above air gradually began to fill my lungs. While it was poison to most, we were immune, and the cold sharpness it held was nice. The air in the bunker was always warm.

We reached the surface and saw a large yellow school bus. Like from the movies. I gasped as Milton honked from the horn from the driver's side.

"All aboard? Who wants to go to Risky Rush Amusement Park?"

Risky Rush Amusement Park? I looked to my friends, who were grinning ear to ear. Everyone hurried to the bus and got on. I had just made it up the stairs when I stopped short.

Cal.

"Why are you here?" I demanded, reading his name tag. Callahan Gorland. My worst enemy. He was sitting directly behind Milton.

"I thought the same thing." He glared at the back of Milton's chair and kicked it.

"I needed a hand to make sure everything was safe, doll." Milton winked at me through his mask. "Couldn't have the birthday girl's special day be ruined by a couple of creepies or crawlies."

I reluctantly sat on the other side of the aisle, still close to Milton. Once we were all inside, he closed the door, turned the radio on, and started off.

"You can stop staring, birthday girl. I don't give two shits about you," he said when I kept glaring at him. I turned away, giving him the middle finger. Despite being trained differently, all of us had been brought up in the same bunker and knew each other too well. And I knew I hated Callahan.

We drove on into the night, finally coming upon an old, abandoned theme park. Risky Rush Amusement Park, read the rusty, decrepit sign that had been welded onto another sign.

"Is it safe?" I asked.

Everybody laughed.

"Nothing in the above world is safe," Pearl said, "but it sure as hell is fun."

Milton parked, and we got off the bus, running inside the park.

Woah.

"Just wait." Milton placed his arm around me when I stood there, frozen. "Cal, will you do the honors?"

"You're going to get us killed," Cal muttered and stormed off. A moment later, there was a loud click and the entire park whirred to life. Carnival music and yellow lights invaded my brain. The carousel moved and a roller coaster dove down its track.

"Happy birthday, Eleanor. Be safe."

I spun around at the familiar voice. My Daddy stood there with a large gun slung over his shoulder.

"I thought—"

"You're the last Young Lady in your group. We wanted to do something special. To turn on the power, we needed more Daddies on sight. Go, have fun." He waved me off. I threw my arms around him and ran off.

I caught up with my friends at the ride labeled "Tilt-A-Whirl". I climbed into the shell-shaped container and rode with my friends. We screamed as loud as we could as the ride jerked to life and spun us around and around!

We moved from ride to ride, laughing and talking loudly, as if... as if we were normal. As if the world hadn't been bombed decades ago, forcing us to go underground. To stay trapped in time. No, for just one evening, we were just modern teenagers, with no duties to help mankind. We could just live.

"You guys go on ahead. Ride the Cyclone." I waved them off, feeling queasy, when they took the roller coaster for the third time, and they hurried to go again. I rested along the rusted metal rails when a DIT sauntered over. By his gait, I knew it was Cal. I rolled my eyes and turned away.

"How's it going, birthday girl?"

Callahan was too handsome for his own good. His hazel eyes shone through the mask, twinkling with overconfidence. I was the only Young Lady who hadn't fallen head over heels for his muscular frame, handsome features, and perfect, charming smile.

"It's fine," I said curtly, hating his smile.

"Did you get everything you wanted?"

I eyed him with suspicion. Why was he acting nice? Cal had never been nice to me.

"Mostly." I sighed. Everything but time with Milton. He'd gone on a few rides but had been pulled to help walk the perimeter with the other Daddies. It looked like I wasn't getting the only thing I had truly wanted for today.

"You like Milton," Callahan said firmly, as if reading my thoughts.

"It's not a crime," I said, crossing my arms defensively, "to have a crush."

"No, but him acting on them is. You know he can't date you. Why even risk it?"

The rules for the bunker were stupid. Young Ladies were to stay celibate until their duties were done, then they'd be artificially inseminated in a doctor's office and give birth to the next generation. But then what? They refused to tell us what happened after.

"What kind of life is this?" I huffed, looking up at him. "You ever want to do more than just your duties to mankind?"

"Like what?" he asked.

"I don't know. Go to dances, first dates, and stuff like they did before the bombs. Get married, and—"

"Have sex?" He smirked.

I glared at him. "Yes. All of it. I want more than what the bunker has to offer. Is that so bad?"

Cal cleared his throat to speak, but was interrupted by a slew of gunshots just outside the gates. Shouting incurred, and we shared a look as more guns went off.

Oh, no. We'd drawn them out.

Rule Three - Callahan
Don't rat on your fellow DIT's.

"What happened, soldiers?" Cecil, the warden for the DITs, barked, when the door to the rec hall slammed closed.

When we stayed silent, Cecil growled, "Someone better fucking speak. We have a Daddy dead and a DIT missing. What the fuck happened out there?"

Silence.

"Well then. If no one is going to explain, then we'll just have to deal with the consequences. There'll be no more alcohol, cigarettes, and no excursions until we get some answers."

Lewis bolted up. "Sir, we had nothing to do with the crawlie attack. We did our best out there. I need my smokes."

Cecil clicked his tongue. "I see, now we know something. It was a crawlie attack?"

"Yes, sir," Lewis responded. My jaw tightened, and I fought back the urge to kick the back of his calf and knock him to his knees. Fucking rat bastard.

"And where were all of you?" Cecil paced as he interrogated us. The warden was one of the first children in the bunker. He still remembered what it was like before the bombs, and he never let us forget it. "Because it looks like you just let Dale get murdered in cold blood by one of those pumped-up, radiation-filled monsters, and our best and brightest DIT was taken. How many were there?"

"Too many for us to fight off. We barely got the girls back to the bus," Russel said. "I don't know where they came from. I've never seen that many in one place."

"Did you deviate from the approved plans?" Cecil demanded. All of us tightened our lips. If the warden found out that we'd found a way to turn the power back on, he'd whip our bare asses until one of us closed our eyes for good. I kicked Lewis, still standing.

"No, sir. Everything was going just as planned," he answered.

"And no one knows where Milton went?" Cecil shook his head. While we weren't allowed to know who our biological parents were, it was suspected that Milton and Cecil were related. Not only was he undeservedly at the top of our class, but the physical resemblances were too many to not draw conclusions. Any of us could have died and it wouldn't have been a big deal, but it wasn't just anyone. It was Milton.

"What's going to happen now?" Russell asked. "We're sorry, sir."

"Sorry doesn't bring back Dale or Milton," Cecil barked. "Sorry doesn't fix the fact that we now have a Young Lady without a Daddy, and there's none left from that group to replace him. Eleanor is the best collector, you fucking idiots!" Spit flew out of his mouth and his face grew red with fury.

He went on for hours, screaming and demanding that we go through everything we did tonight, starting with me and Milton going up first to get the bus and secure the park.

"We did everything by the book, sir," I said. "There wasn't a creepie in sight."

It wasn't until Dorothy, the den mother for the Young Ladies, came in, that Cecil finally let us go.

"Back to your rooms, soldiers. Get some rest. Tomorrow, we start search-and-rescue missions. We're not stopping until we have a body. Alive or dead." The room was silent until Cecil and Dorothy left. Then, the room erupted.

"Search and rescue? He wants us to go into a creepie den? Or worse, a crawlie cave?" Harold shuddered. "I can't do it, man. I vowed to serve, but I'm not going to get myself killed."

"Milton might as well be dead if he ain't already," Carl added. "A search-and-rescue mission is ridiculous at this point."

"Can't we just tell them the truth?" Sam asked. All of us turned to him and he shrunk into his seat.

"No," I said firmly. "We are all going to do exactly as we'd discussed on the way back. We're going to keep our fucking mouths shut, go about our business, and move on. It'll pass, and they'll figure things out. This isn't the first Daddy to get lost above."

"And Eleanor, what are they going to do with her? What about Milton's Young Lady-in-Training? Now, she has no one when she comes of age," Russell said.

"She just won't be picked. Sorry about her luck." I shrugged. The little tyke, whoever it may be, was better off being put in Gen Pop anyway. Being picked to be a Young Lady or a Daddy wasn't all it cracked up to be. My last conversation with Eleanor before the gunshots echoed in my mind.

She didn't want to be a Young Lady anymore. Now, she was free.

I looked back at the men whom I'd known since childhood. All of us were just indoctrinated bodies to be thrown against the wars waging above. Despite being told we were the elite, the best of the best, we weren't shit to them. Cecil,

Dorothy, and all the other leaders were just as brainwashed as everyone else. I refused to let myself be one of them.

"Come on, let's go to bed. It's been a long fucking night," I told my fellow DITs.

With our shoulders slumped and eyes heavy, we marched back to our floor and then to our rooms.

I showered and went to bed, and as much as I tried to sleep, my mind kept drifting back to Eleanor. The birthday girl.

I'd been reluctant to put all this shit on tonight. In fact, I was downright against it all. Eleanor was a spoiled brat, worse than all the other Young Ladies. She was one of the best collectors, and she knew it. Her better-than-me attitude drove me nuts, and I promised myself that whatever Young Lady was assigned to me in a few years would never act like that.

I hated her, and let her know it. But Milton, my best friend, didn't think like I did. He saw a cute face and a slender yet curvy frame. Sure, she was gorgeous, but she was spoiled. I couldn't look past that. He'd been crushing on Eleanor for years, and he'd begged me to help him declare those feelings today.

And what did that get him?

Lost.

Left for dead.

Probably dead.

Hopefully dead.

Milton was just another run-of-the-mill Daddy. Not a unique thought in his head. He didn't need one. He was Cecil's grandson, probably. He didn't need to figure a way out of this place.

As my body finally gave in to sleep, my last thoughts were of Eleanor, and how she would take the news tomorrow. She and the other Young Ladies had been taken back long before we climbed down into the bunker tonight. Did she know that both her Daddy and her boyfriend were gone? What would she do?

Rule Four - Callahan
Karma can be a bitch.

One month later.

"Soldiers, we've made a decision." Cecil stormed into the rec hall carrying his clipboard. This was the first time in weeks we'd had a moment to relax. "We are officially ceasing all missions for Milton. We need to resume collecting. However, if upon your regular training missions, you come upon any hint or clue of Milton's whereabouts, dead or alive, you are fully expected to report your findings directly to me."

We exchanged silent looks. It was a fine line. On one hand, we were relieved to be done running twelve-hour missions up above, knowing we weren't going to find anything. On the other, Milton was Cecil's bloodline, and acting too excited to stop looking for him would get us beaten.

"You will resume your training tomorrow. Well, all but one of you."

Confused murmurs flooded the room, and Cecil cleared his throat.

"The decision has been made that one of you will be moved up, replacing Dale as Eleanor's Daddy."

The room erupted into mixed comments.

"Sir, this has never been done before."

"Whoever gets paired with her is not going to have that parental-like bond with her."

"She's a bitch." The room stopped abruptly, my comment echoing throughout the room. I shrugged innocently. It was true.

Ever since Eleanor's Daddy died, she'd been insufferable. Cutting the line at mealtimes, bawling loudly in the halls. She'd been using the excuse that she was grieving over the loss of her Daddy as a reason to be an absolute... cunt.

"Bro," Russell scolded, "you can't say that."

"Why not?" I stood up. "She is. She's always been this way, and now, it's just gotten worse. Whoever gets assigned to her is going to be fucking miserable."

"Oh, how ironic," Cecil said with a disgusting grin. He raised his clipboard and tugged a manila folder from the clip. "Congratulations, Callahan, you're a Daddy."

∽

"This is absolute bullshit!" I shouted at Cecil and Dorothy when his office door was slammed shut. "Why me?"

Dorothy took the folder from Cecil and began flipping through the large stack of papers.

"You're top of your class. Your marks were all better than Milton's." She gave a side glance to Cecil. "Your trainers all list you as the best marksman with both a gun and a knife. You have the highest kill count of all the DITs. Frankly, you're the only one we can trust to handle Eleanor."

"There's no handling that girl." I shook my head. "She may be a Young Lady, legally an adult, but she's got the personality of a spoiled eight year old."

Cecil sat behind his desk, facing me. We stared at each other a moment before he burst into laughter.

"What?" I demanded.

"And you think your attitude is much better? Son, I have watched you grow up here in the bunker, and you are just as bad as her. I tried to persuade Ms. Dorothy not to pick you because of how you two fight, but she insisted the paperwork doesn't lie."

"It doesn't. You're the best for this job," she insisted.

"She's going to get me killed too." I leaned forward, gripping the arms of the chair. "With all due respect, sir, you make me go above with her and one of us ain't coming back."

"Is that a threat?" He stood, looming over me. "This isn't a game, Callahan. It's been decided. They're stripping your quarters as we speak and moving you up to her floor. You don't have a say in this."

He leaned forward, his face so close to mine I could smell his toothpaste and the whiskey on his breath. "And if you let her die, your fate will be worse."

"Yes, sir."

I'd heard horror stories about what they did to people who they deemed punishable past death. They'd be pushed above, with no PARA suit or gas mask, and left to the elements. Without anything to protect them from the chemicals in the air, they wouldn't die; they'd turn into a creepie or a crawlie.

"I have one request, sir."

Cecil sat back down. "And that is?"

"Let me clean up my own space."

He raised an eyebrow. "Contraband?"

"I am a young man, sir."

He laughed and slid his hand over to the telephone. "You got a hold of a magazine from above, didn't you? It's okay, I have a small stack myself." He picked up his phone and called someone, giving orders for them to leave my room alone.

"Anything else?"

"No, sir. But I still don't think this is going to work. Eleanor is beyond my capabilities."

"See, this is where I have to disagree with you, son. You're her Daddy now. Use your power of authority to wrangle her in some."

"How do you suppose I do that?" I scoffed.

"What have you been taught to do if your young girl is being disobedient?"

"Punish her. But, sir—"

"Then you punish her."

I rolled my eyes. "I can't put her in a corner."

"Why not?"

I looked from him to Dorothy. She nodded. Did they expect me to treat Eleanor like a petulant child?

Cecil cleared his throat. "When this idea was brought to me last week, I had the same worries you have right now. When you are assigned your Young Ladies, the goal is for them to look at you as a parental-like figure, and to develop a bond with one another. A father-daughter type of relationship. But you didn't have that opportunity with Eleanor. So, you'll have to do a speed course through it."

"What does that mean?" I asked.

"It means, treat her like you'd treat the child you'd just been assigned. Give her love and affection when she's good and punish her when she's not. You've trained for what, eleven, twelve years now? How old are you, son?"

"I'm twenty."

"Yes, so your training is almost done anyway. You know exactly what to do with her. If you are stuck, bring out the manual. There's no shame in double-checking."

"I think you underestimate Eleanor's stubbornness."

"I think you overestimate how much I give a shit about what you think." Cecil walked around the desk. "My Young Lady, Myrtle, was quite similar to Eleanor. Sharp-tongued but good at what she did. She learned quickly that the Young Ladies who did well were treated better, given more CAFE bucks, more presents, more treats. But she struggled with listening. The moment those doors closed, and all the people who adored her couldn't see her anymore, she became nasty, mean, and lazy."

"I remember Myrtle," Dorothy added.

"Yes. Myrtle was special. One time, I asked her to pick up after herself and she bit me."

"She bit you?"

He nodded. "She did. And I'll never forget the look on her pretty little face when I scooped her up, lifted her skirt, and beat her ass until it was purple. Oh, how she howled and kicked and clawed at me, begging me to stop, but every time I did, she would just go right back to her awful behavior, so I'd do it again. Then finally, one day, she stopped."

Cecil went behind his desk again and rifled through his drawers. "She was still feisty, but now she was well-behaved. We had a wonderful relationship after that." He pulled out a small black book and flipped through the pages. "So believe me when I say I know exactly what you're going through."

"What happened to her?" I asked. No one really knew what happened to the Young Ladies after they aged out. Retired Daddies were tasked with training the new DITs. But no one ever saw the Young Ladies again once they'd been impregnated. Cecil pulled out a slip of paper and handed it to me. It was a photo of a beautiful young woman, who looked vaguely familiar.

"She aged out, was taken to the doctors for seed implementation, and nine months later, she became Eleanor's biological mother."

Rule Five - Eleanor
Throwing a fit will get you nowhere.

"Eleanor, we have news."

I bolted up from my bed. "You found Milton?" My chest swelled with hope. It'd been weeks, sending Daddies and DITs out to try to find him only to come back to the bunker empty. They had to know something.

"No." Dorothy sniffed the air in my bedroom and made a sour face. "I want you to shower, take care of whatever is making this room smell this way, and get everything picture-perfect clean. You've been reassigned."

"Reassigned? What does that mean?"

"You have a new Daddy. He is on his way up now. Thankfully, your Daddy's room does not smell like this one does." She nodded to the door on the right wall. On the other side was my Daddy's room. They'd cleaned it out the day after my birthday, leaving no trace of the Daddy that had been killed in action.

My Daddy. His name was Dale.

"How can I just get a new one? That doesn't make sense!" I leapt out of bed. "I don't want a new Daddy."

"Yes, well, we didn't want your original one to be torn in

half by crawlies either, did we?" she retorted. "Shower, clean, and prepare. Your new Daddy will be here by dinner."

Begrudgingly, I scrubbed my body, washed my hair, and when I got out, I stared in the mirror. I looked like a shell of the Young Lady I was just a month ago. My eyes were tired, my smile gone, and despite having Hispanic genes that made my skin tan, I was pale.

I needed to go above. Get some non-bunker air. Even the chemically stained air above was better than the stale stuff down here. A small chime rang in the bathroom, reminding me to take my pills. We weren't allowed to know what the pills were, but they did a multitude of things for us. Kept our bodies hairless, except for the hair on our heads and eyebrows, and helped us maintain a healthy weight in the event we couldn't get enough nutrition from our food. It kept our cycles regular with only a light flow. The pills made our muscles strong, our lungs and hearts strong, and most importantly, our minds. They made us perfect Young Ladies.

I recited the little commercial that played on the TV regularly in my head and then took a pill. It was the least I could do for myself as I'd neglected everything else.

I cleaned my room and waited patiently for my new Daddy to arrive. Would I be given a retired one? One of the older Daddies who'd already had a Young Lady and done their time above? I tried to rack my brain, remembering each one. There weren't many, though.

I wrung my hands and tapped my feet until there was a knock, right before dinner time, and the door slid open, revealing Dorothy.

"Eleanor, your new Daddy is here. Please stand."

When I stood, Dorothy stepped aside and everything around me started to spin. No. No, it couldn't be! Never in a million years would I have thought that it would be Callahan.

I let out a small shriek as my vision blurred and the room went dark, and then black altogether.

∼

A cold rag on my forehead brought me back to consciousness.

"Huh?" I asked, blinking rapidly. "What happened?"

Dorothy and one of the bunker medics stood beside the bed, staring at me with concern. "You fainted. Are you okay?" Dorothy asked.

I sat up slowly and looked around. My room was clean. And it smelled of fresh soap.

"Why did I faint? Did something happen? Did you find Milton?" I looked around hopefully, and then my mood plummeted when I saw someone sitting in a chair to the side. It felt like I ran right into a brick wall made of my most recent memories. Callahan, my worst enemy, had been assigned to be my Daddy.

"No. You can't do this," I protested.

"Sshh..." Dorothy pet my hair and urged me to lay back down. "We can, and we have. The decision has been made. Your new Daddy has already moved into his room alongside yours and will begin accompanying you on missions above. We know this is untraditional, but considering the circumstances, we had little choice but to move one of our DITs up."

I closed my eyes but continued to argue, "Please, no."

"Rest. It's time to start the healing process, sweetie. Callahan is your new Daddy, and you will need to treat him with just as much respect as you did your previous one."

"Why? I hate him." I knew I sounded like a child, but I didn't care. They had no idea what it felt like. What I was going through. I lost the only person who maybe loved me, and the only boy who maybe liked me. All in one night. I had to grieve over the loss of my Daddy and my someday-boyfriend at the same time. It wasn't fair to add more fuel to this raging fire pit of despair!

"In time, you'll grow to love him just as you had your other Daddy," Dorothy assured me, but I didn't believe her. My Daddy and I had a special bond. He was the only adult who showed me any sort of affection past stiff politeness. Even Dorothy was cold to us most of the time. This was unusual for her.

"And until then, what am I supposed to do?" I sat up and crossed my arms. "Just pretend he's not the same age as me? That he's an authoritative figure? I couldn't listen to him if I tried." I glared at him from across the room. Callahan's face was blank, as if bored. Bored!

"You wanted this, didn't you?" I pointed and accused. "You love seeing me at my lowest. I bet you love knowing that I was stripped of everyone I cared about, don't you?"

"Eleanor," Dorothy warned. "That's not the way to speak to your Daddy."

"Or what?" I mocked. "He'll punish me? Too late for that, buddy. My old Daddy couldn't break me. There's no way you're going to."

Callahan leaned forward, clapping his hands slowly. "You really are quite the drama queen."

"Why you—" I leapt up and lunged for him. Dorothy and the medic snatched me back. Suddenly, something was being plunged into my arm, and I gasped with pain.

"You have disappointed me today, Eleanor," Dorothy said after I was dragged back to bed. My head was dizzy, and I could barely keep my eyes open. Those bastards had sedated me. "Whether you like it or not, we have to continue. For the human race to one day thrive and leave the bunker, we must continue to send you out to collect the necessary items to help us create a solution."

I raised my arms, which felt like limp noodles. "Just give

everyone the pills." I said, my vision going blurry. I was going to fall asleep. I wobbled on my feet. "There's tons of them. I've seen it." I struggled to get my words out, my tongue and everything else feeling heavy.

A hand slapped over my mouth. "Don't listen to her, she's delusional." She urged my head back to my pillow. I was so weak from the sedatives, I couldn't fight, and quickly lay back, defeated. Why wasn't Callahan supposed to know about the pills? I wanted to ask, but my mouth was dry and my jaw felt too heavy to form words.

"Callahan, stay with her tonight. If she gets up, assist her. The sedatives were heavy."

While I couldn't do anything but listen, I heard them leave my room. A chair scooted closer, and I felt hot air on my cheek. I groaned and turned slowly away.

"Hello, Young Lady," Callahan said dryly.

"Cal." The word was heavy, but I managed to get it out. I wanted to scream and shout and kick and thrash like a toddler denied dessert, but it was futile. Our fates had been decided, and I had no say in the matter.

"Nuh-uh." His voice took on a sing-song tone, and he tsked. "That's not my name anymore, is it? Oh, sweet Eleanor. Sweet, sweet, cunty Eleanor, you have to call me Daddy."

Rule Six - Eleanor
Listen to your Daddy the first time.

"What happened last night?" Frances asked as we made our way through the breakfast line. "You look awful."

I swung my head over to her. "Thanks," I said sarcastically. "I got reassigned."

"Reassigned? What do you mean?" We got our oatmeal and toast and went to sit with the other Young Ladies.

"It means, I got reassigned to someone else." I grit my teeth and kept my head down.

"I don't understand. Are you leaving us?" Olive asked, her voice panicked. We'd all been in a state of confusion and worry since my Daddy died. Well, now we knew. If your Daddy dies, you just get a new one.

"No." A hand on my shoulder caused me to jerk forward. "Eleanor is staying here with all the other Young Ladies. She's been reassigned to me," Callahan explained. I brushed off his hand.

"Don't touch me."

He chuckled and started off toward the other Daddies. They had their breakfast in another area and had already eaten. They were chatting and smiling, welcoming Callahan into the fray. He looked so out of place with them. The other Daddies were ten years older than him.

"Callahan is your Daddy?" Frances gaped. "How?"

"Beats me," I snapped. "I don't want to talk about it."

"We have to talk about this," Olive insisted. "How long have you known?"

"I didn't know anything. They just moved him in."

"When? Last night?" Nancy screeched.

"Yes. Now shut it." I stabbed my oatmeal.

"Oh, I'm so jealous!" Nancy continued. "Callahan, out of all the DITs? You're so lucky, Eleanor. He's ridiculously handsome. And you get to see him every day! You get to live with him?" She lowered her voice to a whisper, "Have you seen him naked?"

"No!" I slid my bowl away. "Why would I? Have you seen your Daddy naked? Nancy, you're disgusting."

I glanced up at the men on the other side. Callahan was watching me. His hazel eyes made contact with my brown ones. He tilted his coffee cup to me, and I flipped him off. The table gasped at my act of defiance.

"Eleanor, what are you doing? You can't do that!" Pearl shoved my hand down.

"Why not? Everyone is breaking rules, apparently. If they think I'll be treating him like I did my old Daddy, they're dead wrong."

Callahan shook his head at me. I flipped him off again but Pearl caught me mid-bird and covered it.

"You're going to get yourself in trouble."

"Trouble?" I laughed. "If I was going to get into trouble, it would have been for any of the things I've done before. Not for giving Callahan the middle finger."

"Are you still allowed to call him that?" Olive snickered. "I've never called my Daddy by his name."

Like Father, Like Slaughter

"Why wouldn't I?" I gave her a pointed look.

"Because there are rules," Pearl protested. "Young or not, if he's been assigned to you, then you have to treat him just as you had your... other Daddy."

"I don't care what they want." I stared at my breakfast, teary-eyed. I'd barely taken three bites, but I felt sick. I couldn't sit here anymore. I stood and took my tray to the trash. I passed by the Daddies, pausing at Callahan. I looked back at my friends. "I'll never call him by his title."

I stormed out of breakfast with my head high. They could force me to work with him, but I'd be damned if I treated him like my elder.

"Hey! Where are you going, Young Lady?" The doors behind me were thrown open and I turned my head to see Callahan storming out after me.

"I'm going to find somewhere to hide from you. We don't need to be together all the time."

"You know the rules, Eleanor. If you are in public, you need an escort." He jogged to me and put his hand on my elbow. "It's unsafe."

"What do you think will happen? All the baddies are above us," I pointed out. "No one's going to hurt me here."

His eyes darkened and the corner of his mouth twitched. "Baddies are everywhere. Eleanor, this isn't ideal for either of us, but we have to get over it. I'm your Daddy, and you're my Young Lady. You need to respect me and call me by my title."

"Like hell. I'd rather be ripped in half by crawlies and fed to the creepies than call you anything other than Callahan. Leave me alone, and I'll do the same to you." I poked his chest and stormed to my room. As soon as the door slid down, I threw myself onto my bed and burst into tears. This couldn't be happening!

My friends' reactions at the table made everything so much worse. The way they were excited. Excited? How could anyone be thrilled about this situation? This was literally the worst. Being attractive didn't make up for how rude and mean and downright cruel he'd been to me for the last ten years. His handsome face was a disguise. I bet he'd planned all of this. That's why he volunteered to help with my birthday celebration above.

I sat up. How had I not realized it before? He wanted to torture me further. And for what? I'd never done anything to him, other than get picked to be a Young Lady. My door opened and Callahan stepped inside.

"I don't appreciate you acting like that in public, Eleanor."

I laughed. "Like what? Like I'm upset? Like I'm angry?"

"Like a child."

"A child?" I scoffed and slid off my bed. I stormed across the room and shoved his chest, forcing him back. "A child? That's just it. I'm not. I don't need anyone watching over me, and even if I did, I certainly wouldn't want it to be you."

"I can do the job just as well as any of the other ones. I was top in my class. Even higher than your boyfriend." He snickered. "Milton was just a pretty face."

"Don't speak his name." I poked him again.

"Why? He was my best friend. You want to know the truth? He was going to fuck you and toss you away."

Tears spilled from my eyes. "T-that's not true."

"Oh yes, it is." He touched my shoulders and urged me back. "He didn't care about you. He couldn't. Milton had no feelings."

"Stop talking like he's dead!" I put my hands over my ears. "You're just jealous because no one could ever like you as much as they liked him. You're an ass, and you'll never be my Daddy!"

In a flash, I was scooped up and Callahan strode over to my bed. I kicked and fought but his grip was tight as he tossed me over his lap.

"You know what?" he said and lifted my dress. "The warden warned me you'd be a little brat and told me to treat you exactly as I would if we'd been assigned to each other earlier. I don't think time-outs are going to work with you, Eleanor."

"What are you doing?" I tried to pull my skirt down, but the more I fought, the angrier he became. Callahan brought his hand down on my bottom.

I screamed.

"Stop! Callahan!" The tears for Milton turned into tears for myself and the humiliation.

"That's not my name," he growled.

"I'm not saying it."

"Fine." He spanked me again. I pressed my lips tightly and closed my eyes. I could zone out until he was done. He'd break before me. Another hard spank and when I didn't give him any reaction, he shifted. Rough fingers hooked the sides of my panties and before I could protest, he ripped them down my bottom and halfway down my thighs.

"No!" I squirmed, but he tightened his hold.

"You want to act like a brat, you'll be treated like one. What's my name?"

"Callahan."

Smack!

The collision of skin on skin hurt ten times more than with the thin layer of cotton to shield my behind. I sobbed. He asked again, and through my tears, I answered, "Callahan."

He spanked me. Over and over, each time repeating his question. I wasn't going to break. I refused to give in to his ridiculous demand.

"Your skin is turning purple." He ran his hand over my bruised ass, and I flinched. He slowly trailed it down the, freezing at the spot that would take this from punishment to...

My heart raced as his hand stayed there, resting on the spot right before my sex. I was in pain, extreme pain, but yet...

"What is my name?" he asked.

I lifted my head, ready to fight again. Then he raised his hand and my head fell in defeat.

"Daddy."

Rule Seven - Callahan
Take care of your Young Lady.

What had I done? I stared at my hands as I paced my private quarters. Eleanor was currently in her room, whimpering from the pain. I'd been so angry, so fucking angry, that I'd blacked out. I'd bent her over my knee and spanked her. But that wasn't what had me so concerned. What worried me the most was that I had no memory of pulling down her underwear, and I couldn't get rid of this hard-on.

Had she noticed? How long had I been hard while having her on my lap? Why did I like it so much? The image of her bare ass filled my mind. I had wanted to explore all of her. One quick slip of my finger and I could have...

No!

Young Ladies were off-limits. It was disgusting. I was a predator. The things they'd hammered into us for the last ten years.

Don't touch the Young Ladies.

Not in the way I'd almost done tonight.

I closed my eyes and tried to focus on something else, anything else, but Eleanor's soft crying from the other room made it hard. It made everything hard. Despite myself, my hand drifted to my cock. I massaged myself through my pants and swore. What had I done? Pulling myself out of the hypnotic fixation, I stormed back into her room.

"What do you want?" she demanded through her sobs. "Get out."

"I want to see your bruise."

"Why? So you can brag to all the other Daddies what you did to me?" She turned her head away, her body remaining in place. She couldn't lay on her back. I moved closer to the bed. She'd pulled her underwear back up. Cautiously, I touched her skirt.

"I just want to see the bruise."

"You're sick," she said but didn't fight me as I gingerly lifted the layers of her clothing to see the deep purple of her behind. Well, fuck. I stormed out, heading to the medical center. The attendant eyed me up and down as I asked for arnica cream, but gave it to me anyway. I went back to her room and sat at the edge of her bed.

"I'm going to touch you now," I warned, lifting her skirt.

"Haven't you done enough, Daddy?" she spat. "You're worse than I thought."

My hands trembled as I put both hands on her hips, sliding her underwear down. She winced, and I lifted the cotton fabric gingerly.

"My job as a Daddy isn't just to punish you when you get out of line but to take care of you and make sure you're happy, healthy, and safe."

"Well, I don't feel any of those things." She tried to fight me as I pulled her underwear all the way off. It was probably best she didn't have anything against her skin for a day or so. I cleared my throat nervously as I stared at her swollen ass.

"I have a cream that's going to help heal you. It's cold." I unscrewed the lid and dipped my fingers into the white lotion.

My mouth watered as I brought my hand to her backside and began to slowly, carefully, rub the soothing lotion in.

She winced.

"Shh, let Daddy take care of you." The word felt foreign and confusing on my tongue, but she let out a small moan and my cock jumped to attention. Thankfully, her head was turned away from me.

"I didn't mean to hurt you so bad," I relented as I continued to massage her. Her ass cheeks were so soft and plump. I shifted my body, and in doing so, gave myself the best view of her lips from behind. Oh, how easy it'd be to simply slip inside and explore.

Eleanor winced, whimpered, and occasionally moaned. All of which made my cock twitch and strain against my pants.

"You're beautiful. I should have never taken to corporal punishment," I said as I ran a finger along her slit. I'd heard about men using the other hole. They'd claimed it was tighter, better than the one more commonly accepted. Would that keep her virginity intact?

No one would have to know.

"Eleanor?" I whispered. She didn't reply, so I called her name again. "Eleanor?"

"Yes, Daddy?"

My cock wept. I stared at her head for a long time. She was not going to look in my direction. I'd hurt her. Growing bold, I cleared my throat loudly, and as I did so, I unzipped my pants and pulled out my rigid length. I was a deviant, preying on this Young Lady's pain. Seeing her flinch and moan only made me harder. I ran my slick, lotion-covered hand over her ass. I stroked myself as I slid between her cheeks. She jumped but didn't try to fight me. I wasn't sure if it was because I now scared her, or if she was enjoying herself as much as I was.

I closed my eyes and imagined how good it would feel to move between her thighs and slide my cock up and down her ass, eventually positioning myself right at her tight little hole. The one that wouldn't expose our secret. I ran my finger against the wrinkled spot, and she tightened, making me pull back.

"I won't hurt you," I told her. "I just want you to feel better." I dipped my hand back into the jar and lathered another layer onto her bruised bottom. Oh, how tight her pussy must be. I'd been down to the Gen Pop bars with the other DITs to have fun, but those women weren't new to sex. Hell, some of them had made it their careers, according to Milton, who enjoyed their services often. None of them mattered though. I'd never truly wanted any of them the way I wanted Eleanor right now.

Daring it, my finger ran down, tracing her bare pussy lips. She let out a small gasp. I trailed all the way up to her mound, and then back down again, teasing myself and her, but not pushing between her folds. I did it again at a lazy pace, all while continuing to stroke myself. No one had ever been here before, touching her like this. The very idea spurred me on. I wanted to be the first to touch, to taste, and to fuck her.

The second time my finger ran along her slit, her hips shifted upward ever so slightly. What was this? A gift? A request?

"Daddy?" she asked.

"Yes, Eleanor?" I squeezed my cock, slick with precum.

"Are you going to make me feel better?"

I bit down. Oh, her voice was so... needy.

"Yes. I can do that. I can make you feel good if you want. Do you want that, Eleanor?" There was a pause, and then she said.

"Yes, Daddy."

I slid my pointer finger between her lips and found her soaking wet. She gasped as I ran along her slit, finding her clit easily.

"This will make you feel good. You just need to relax."

I stroked her wet, velvet folds tenderly. I explored her with a hunger I'd never felt before. God, how beautiful she was. She'd always been prettier than the other Young Ladies, but now, now she was otherworldly, splayed out with her ass in the air and her pussy on display for me to stroke as slow or as fast as I wanted. I matched her breathing cadences. She squirmed restlessly and gripped the sheets. Her breaths turned into pants and the hand stroking my member matched the speed at which my fingers strummed her clit.

"Oh, Daddy!" Eleanor cried out as she jerked and came all over my fingers. Her body pulsed, growing wetter and warmer. Her words had sent me over the edge as well, and I came in my hand. I opened my eyes once I came down, and stared at my hand, covered in my cum. What did I do? I gulped and removed the hand from between her legs.

"Do you feel better now?" I asked.

"Yes, Daddy."

With shaky hands, I dipped both into the jar, mixing my fluids with the arnica cream. I spread them around my hand, mixing them thoroughly and returned to her purple ass. "Just one more layer and then rest." I rubbed the concoction over her, admiring every curve and mark. I'd never seen such a beautiful thing as Eleanor orgasming. I wanted to experience it as much as possible if I could.

Post-come clarity hit me all of a sudden, as I finished spreading the lotion. I pulled back in disgust at myself. This wasn't the man I was twenty-four hours ago. This was someone entirely different. I was someone's Daddy now.

What had I just done to my Young Lady?

Rule Eight - Callahan
Protect your Young Lady at all costs.

We didn't speak about what happened the next morning. In fact, we didn't speak at all. I couldn't read her. Was she upset, embarrassed, angry? I was all three at myself.

I should have never let my devious desires interfere with my job. She was a Young Lady, and I was her Daddy. I was to be dedicated, attentive, devoted, and a defender of my Young Lady. Not her lover.

I followed her dutifully for the next week, like all the other Daddies. Unless we were on a mission above, most of our time was spent simply watching from a short distance to make sure they weren't doing or saying something they shouldn't be. What that could even possibly be was beyond me, but I did as I'd been trained.

The other Daddies, my seniors, were nice enough. They knew I knew their secret, the truth about what happened the night of Eleanor's birthday, and could rat them out any second. Instead of being shitty to me, they chose to befriend me. They made jokes and invited me to have coffee in the morning and drinks at dinner. Despite all the attempted distractions, I was sweating bullets from morning 'til night, when we'd return to our rooms.

Every time Eleanor spoke to one of her friends, panic shot up my spine. Would she tell them what I did? Which was worse, the brutal spanking or the later abuse of power? What would happen if they found out I broke my oath?

I tried my best to feign calmness. The only time Eleanor left my sight was to use the restroom. While she did call me by my title now, she continued to test my limits in public. I had let it slide for a day or so and then I couldn't take it anymore and began lashing back at her. I threatened another private punishment and while she didn't speak, her eyes told me to bring it on.

She knew I wouldn't do it.

"Eleanor, we should talk," I started, one night after a full week had gone by. We'd made it back to the privacy of her room and I couldn't take it anymore. I needed to know what she thought of me.

"About what?" She didn't look back as she hurried to her bathroom. I opened and shut my mouth. What did that mean? Had I hurt her so badly she'd forgotten; or was she letting me off the hook? I stood there like an idiot for a moment before she turned at the door. "You're fine. I won't tell anyone what you did. Just leave me alone for a while, okay?"

I was taken aback slightly. She was letting this drop. But why? I'd known Eleanor since we were children. She wouldn't do something nice without a motive. She hated me.

"Good night, Daddy. I'm just going to shower, rub some more cream on my bottom, and rest. I'm still sore." She gave me a quick wave and looked at me expectantly. I nodded and went to my room.

I heard her walking in her room and eventually, the shower started. Not being able to get the idea that she was hiding something out of my head, I went back to her room and began to look around. Had she perhaps sent a message to someone using one of the many gadgets Young Ladies had at their disposal?

I searched fast, not knowing how much time I had before she turned the shower off. I reached for her pillow and lifted it, finding a yellow, frayed envelope. I opened the letter and read the contents. My stomach dropped. No. This couldn't be. This made no sense. How? The shower turned off, and I stuffed the letter back and slid it under her pillow. I returned to my room and paced.

While I'd only had the chemically-stained letter in my hand for a brief moment, I was able to memorize what was written.

Eleanor,

I'm alive and safe. I will be waiting every night, where we last saw each other. I'll be hiding in the tram cart number 13. Climb up, meet me, and we can be each other's first time like you wanted. No one has to know.

Love,

Milton.

Love. Ha! Milton didn't love her. And he certainly wasn't a virgin. He'd been the one to take me to the Gen Pop bar in the first place. Initially, I doubted it was him who had written it, but the more I reread it in my mind, the more I was confident it really had been him. Somehow, he'd lasted a full month above ground. How?

It was all coming together now. Eleanor thought she could pull one over on me, but I was one step ahead of her. I started toward the door to confront her, but then realized it would do no good. If she didn't go tonight, she'd try tomorrow, or the next day. She thought Milton loved her, and she was too naive to know it was all a sham. No, I had to let her go and end this for good.

Milton had to be dealt with.

I went to the box I stored in my closet and pulled out a pill bottle. I popped two pills and left my quarters. No one monitored who went in or out these days, so I put on a PARA suit and my gas mask and went out and above. There were plenty of rides to Risky Rush Park. I took one of the motorcycles, leaving Eleanor with a four-wheeler. I rushed to the tram to meet and confront Milton. What state would he be in? He wasn't taking the pills like I was. He had to be...

Despite hating the monster he'd become before the party, I couldn't wish that ill of my old friend. He deserved to die, but not become a creepie. I took the stairs and found tram 13 was still at the gate, and someone was resting against it, waiting.

Milton tilted his head. He looked just as I'd last seen him, except his gas mask had been blackened. I couldn't see his face, but I knew his mannerisms well. There was no doubt in my mind I was staring at my best friend I'd presumed dead.

I presumed that because I was the one who'd left him behind.

"Well, this is a surprise. How did you find out about this?"

"Eleanor was reassigned to me when her Daddy died. What are you doing, Milton?"

"I came to take what was rightfully mine. What would have been, had you left things alone."

When those gunshots had gone off, I ran to help them fight whatever was out there. However once I reached them, I didn't see a single creepie or crawlie in sight. What I found was much worse. Monsters in human skin.

"You're a bastard for agreeing to it," I said.

"You think it was my idea?" Milton kicked off the tram, causing it to rock slightly. "No. They'd been planning this for years. They drew her name out of a hat. Every generation has one. A Young Lady they turn into their whore. She was the one who was supposed to go missing. To not come home that night. Not me!" he screamed and ripped off his helmet.

I shrunk back at the sight of him. Milton's face was covered in purple boils and his hair had fallen out in large chunks, leaving him with bald spots. His eyes were bloodshot and some of the boils were leaking blood and something white. He was turning into a creepie.

I knew it.

"I know you've been taking the pills. Give them to me," he demanded.

"I don't have them. Plus, they don't work like that. You can't fix what's already happened. It's too late."

"Bullshit!" he yelled. "They probably don't work, and that's why you don't want me to have them."

"No," I said, hesitantly. "Given enough time, they do work."

"Prove it. Take your mask off and fight me like a real man."

Reluctantly, I did, tossing the mask next to his black one. I inhaled deeply. I'd never tested the pills out. I was either about to feel fire in my lungs and begin to change, like Milton, or, they were going to work. The air was... okay.

"I'm not going to let you do anything to her."

"Why, because you're her Daddy now?" He laughed. "What are you gonna do, tell on me? She won't believe you. She fucking hates you. I always made sure of that. Remember, when we were kids and you told me how pretty you thought she was? I was jealous. So I did everything I could in that first year to make sure you hated each other. And it worked. Eleanor won't touch you with a ten-foot pole."

"And you think she'll want you? Milton, you're turning." I reached for my gun. "The best thing that could happen to you is for someone to mercy kill you."

"Like hell," he snarled. "I'm going to rip you to pieces with my new-found creepie strength, and then I'm going to put this blackout mask back on and fuck her until I put a bullet in the back of her brain. I think I hear her now." He put his hand over his bleeding ear and grinned. "I do."

Growling, I hurled myself at his middle, dragging him across the platform. We hit the cement half-wall and he pushed me back. I reached for my gun but he was faster than me and managed to slap it out of my hand. I rushed him again, and he flipped over the wall. A sickening slicing sound pierced my ears and I looked over the edge. There were sharp, metal rails strewn all over the park, and Milton had been impaled on two of them. One in his chest, the other through his mouth. I looked away quickly, and just then, I heard Eleanor's voice.

"Milton?" She was coming up the stairs. I panicked, looking around for something, anything to explain why I was here and Milton was not, and then, when I couldn't think of anything, I picked up his blacked-out mask and slid it on, just as she turned the corner and stepped onto the platform.

Shit.

Rule Nine - Eleanor
Breaking curfew is never a good idea.

I'd been hesitant to come. When Olive had handed me the letter in the bathroom, I'd almost tossed it away. But I slid it inside my shirt and went about my day, all the while trying to figure out a plan. My Daddy was too good at his job. He didn't take his eyes off me.

Either that, or he had thoughts about what had happened the night before.

"Milton, is that you?" I crept closer to the masked man, eyeing him up and down. "I thought you died."

He didn't speak.

Oh! I ran to him, throwing myself into his arms. He was alive. I inhaled, only smelling his PARA suit. "How did you manage to survive out here?" I asked. He tilted his head down, but I couldn't see his face. He didn't speak either. "Is your voice box radio broken or something?"

He nodded.

"Oh, how terrible!"

I couldn't imagine being stuck out here in the above world with no way to speak to people. Hesitantly, he put his arms around me and hugged me back, patting me.

"Is there somewhere we can go, where you can take off the mask? It's been weeks. Surely you couldn't survive without removing it to eat."

He shook his head and pointed to me.

Not anywhere I could go.

My mood fell. "Well, I guess I'm glad I get to see you now here. You want to sit down?"

I took his hand and led him to the tram. We stepped inside. This part of the park was relatively untouched by the chemicals and monsters that crept around in the above world. Crawlies must not have found this place yet, and creepies probably wouldn't get too far off the ground.

"Are you going to come back with me? To the bunker?" I asked, hopeful. He shook his head. My stomach twisted. "Is... this the last time I'm going to see you?" There was a hesitance and then a nod.

"Oh, Milton. I wish I could go with you, wherever you're going. It's been awful since you've been gone. My Daddy died the same night you went missing and then they gave me a new one, and, and—" Tears spilled from my eyes. "I hate it!"

He cocked his head.

"You wouldn't believe it. Callahan is my new Daddy. He's even worse than you could even imagine." Should I tell him about what Callahan did after the spanking? I pressed my lips together and shoved the memory down. It would only anger Milton to not have been the first to touch me. "I don't know what to do."

My masked man patted his knee. Cautiously, I sat, and he comforted me as I cried softly against his body. He began to slowly, travel up my thigh and back down, pushing my skirt higher and lower and higher again each time. He shifted me on his lap and something pressed against my bottom, reminding me why I was here in the first place.

Well, why he wanted me here. I came to end things. To say goodbye.

I stared into the mask. I couldn't see anything, not even his eyes. I sighed. I knew it was against the rules, but Milton and I hadn't cared. We'd been fully prepared to take our secret to the grave.

No one had to know.

I swallowed my nerves and slid off his lap.

"Milton, I think this should be the last time we see each other."

He stilled. My heart hammered in my chest as his head dipped.

"This wasn't our plan, I know, but things have changed. It's not romantic anymore, it's... scary," I said, stepping up to him. He spread his legs and pulled me into him. His hands slid up my body, cupping my breasts. I sighed. "Milton."

He fingered the buttons. Slowly, undoing them one by one, he tugged them down. I let him do the same to my brassiere.

My insides were so twisted with nerves, I was on the verge of tears again. With no way to know what he was thinking, I was unsure of what to do. My thoughts kept going to Callahan. He'd be so angry if he caught me right now. He'd kill Milton right here and now, and then punish me when we got back.

Would he make me feel good too?

I looked at myself. My nipples had grown hard and rigid from the shift in temperature.

"We shouldn't keep going," I said, my voice shaking.

He removed his gloves and brought his bare hands to my breasts, running his thumb over my cold nipple. It sent a delightful shiver through me. I closed my eyes and imagined Milton's face inside the mask. However, it morphed into Callahan's, and a moan escaped my throat. If I pretended it was Cal under the mask, I could give Milton what he wanted and then say goodbye for good.

He massaged my breasts, and I let out a groan. I looked at him and then back down at his pants.

He unzipped them and his cock sprung out, thick, long, and impressive. He urged me to sit up slightly and reached for my chin. I smiled up at him, my stomach full of butterflies. He fisted my hair just hard enough to elicit a gasp from me and then he urged me forward, directing my face to his length.

Tentatively, I opened my mouth. He pushed inside of me, and without thinking, almost as if on instinct, I ran my tongue along him and began to suck. A low growl came from him and my heart soared. I grew eager and more dramatic with my motions, taking him all the way to the base, bruising the back of my throat.

My masked lover stretched back and held onto my head, pushing me further and further onto his cock, all the while, I imagined it was Callahan. He pulled my head away from him and stood abruptly then. I looked at him from my knees, and he pulled me to stand. He exposed himself fully and gestured for me to do the same. I started with my skirt, but he shook his head and lifted it, pointing to my panties. I took those off and kicked them with the rest of my clothes.

He sat down and patted his lap. He wanted me to... sit on it? He patted again, and I sidled up, nervously eyeing the part that had just been between my lips. He'd tasted... clean. But how? Where had he found water to bathe up here?

He reached for my hips and positioned me where I needed to be. This was it. I braced myself, closing my eyes. I knew it was going to hurt. Could I handle it? I'd already been bruised so much by Daddy, I mean, Callahan.

Arousal, the same as the night of the spankings, pooled between my legs, and he was able to slide against it, rubbing the tip of it against my sensitive nub. I shivered as he continued doing it, while also massaging and teasing my nipple. I was trying to relax, but I couldn't stop mixing Milton's face with Callahan's, and wondering how he was still so clean after being above for so long. I wanted to ask, but just as I opened my mouth, he moved to my entrance and urged me down.

It was slow, but I screamed out in pain as I tore and bled. I tried to scramble off him, but he held me firm, pushing me down further onto him until my bottom touched his lap. Tears ran down my face from the pain of being stretched like this.

He pushed my head into his neck, and I cried as he moved his hips, jostling me. He moved in and out and it hurt so much each time.

My body clenched around him. It hurt but also felt good. Like I was just on the precipice of pleasure.

"Just let me adjust," I said and ran my hand along his PARA suit. "I wish I could see your face. Your hands and the rest of you seem fine. Could I just see you for a second? Just one little moment?"

He shook his head vehemently, but I reached for his helmet anyway. I couldn't do this without telling him the truth. That I had confusing feelings for his best friend, my mortal enemy and now Daddy. That I wished I hadn't let Milton take my virginity, but that it had been Callahan here instead. I was faster than him and tore the mask off, tossing it to the ground. I looked back at him, and then I screamed.

Rule Ten - Eleanor
Know who you are with at all times.

I fell on the floor. I scurried back, horrified. It wasn't Milton under the mask like I'd been led to believe. It was Callahan.

"Daddy?"

"Eleanor," he hedged. His ash brown hair stuck to his face from the dampness in the mask. His hazel eyes were wide with fear. "Let me explain."

I snatched up my discarded clothing. There was no time for my bra or panties. I pulled on my blouse and shot out of the tram car and across the platform.

"You monster!" I screamed as I rushed down the stairs.

"Eleanor!" he called out, but I moved faster. Fluids ran down my thighs as I fled, but I didn't have time to spare. I had to run.

The stairs were metal, and I didn't have shoes. They poked me as I went down them, but the moment I stepped onto the dirt, I touched glass and fell forward with a sharp cry.

I pulled myself back up and squinted as I brought my foot out into the moonlight. The glass piece was large and only one piece, thankfully, and I dug it out just as he was rounding the last bit of the stairs. We made eye contact and I jumped to my feet, running again.

I couldn't believe I'd put him in my mouth! I'd... enjoyed it and then we... he... I ran through the old, run-down amusement park, past all the rides and games that had given me and my friends such joy just weeks ago. Now everything was terrifying in the darkness.

No wonder he tasted and smelled so clean. He hadn't been out here for weeks. But if he hadn't been Milton, then what had happened to him? It was his handwriting on the letter I'd received. Had my Daddy killed him?

Horror gripped me as I tripped over my feet, causing him to slowly gain on me. I fell completely on my face near the Cyclone roller coaster, and when I got back up and turned to look for him, he was gone. Fear slid up my spine. Not knowing where he was terrified me even more.

I searched for somewhere to hide and saw a dark cavern with a sign that said "Tunnel of love". I ran to it, comforted by the darkness that would shield me from his view. I ducked behind a pillar and looked out. A moment later, he passed by, his head whipping around in search of me.

How was he not wearing a gas mask?

I watched him in fascination. He breathed normally. No disgusting boils or rashes were appearing on his exposed skin. He looked just fine. He turned, and I ducked, but it was too late. He grabbed me from my spot.

"Weren't you taught not to run from your Daddy?" he growled. "You're just one bad thing after another, aren't you, Eleanor? Not respecting me, sneaking out, having sex." My body pulsed with an unusual desire. "I'm going to have to punish you again."

"Haven't you done enough?" I sniffled. My backside flinched. I shook my head. I should have known. I'd been had.

He shook his head. "We've barely gotten started. Tell me,

how should I teach you how to behave? I don't know if a spanking would work this time. I think you need something more."

My body shook with fear as I stared into his intense eyes. He leaned forward and there was a clicking sound before the lights came on inside the ride. I looked past him and saw a large, swan boat floating in water a small distance away. He grinned.

"Let's go for a ride."

He tossed me over his shoulder and deposited me into the boat. He then worked the machine control box and the ride whirred to life. He leapt into the boat, and I found myself trapped with him. His hand went between my legs, pushing my skirt up and exposing myself to him. Blood was still wet on my thighs, the evidence of my stolen virginity.

"That was your first time," he said.

I sniffled and nodded. "It wasn't supposed to be that way."

"How so?" His fingers probed my folds, sliding inside them. I closed my eyes as he began to finger me, lazily swirling small circles around my sensitive bud.

"It was supposed to be with Milton," I whined, pushing him away. He laughed dryly.

"Really, is that why you were trying to break up with him?"

"You're a bastard. We were supposed to be each other's firsts."

He roared with laughter. "You were not his first."

"What? No. We were both virgins."

"Milton absolutely was not." He snickered. His finger slid into my entrance, and I winced. He leaned over, his warm breath heating my neck. "It's better off this way. Milton wouldn't be able to make you come, but I sure as fuck can."

"Fuck you!" I spat and shoved him away.

"Yes, let's do that. Eleanor, be a good girl for Daddy and come sit on my lap."

My core tightened at the use of his title. I shouldn't like that as much as I did. I looked over at him, and he smiled.

"You don't have to close your eyes this time to pretend it's me."

I shivered. He knew? He knew.

"Do as I tell you."

"Yes, Daddy," I whispered.

"What was that?"

"Yes, Daddy," I said, louder.

I stood on the wobbly boat, and he helped me unbutton my blouse. He slid his pants down, revealing his magnificent... cock. I stared at it in disbelief. I'd taken all of that? Daddy leaned forward and licked my nipple. I gasped at the intense sensation as he began to nibble my breast. I arched my back and moved closer to him. This was wrong on so many levels, but it felt too good to stop.

He directed my hips to sit on him, and the second time he pushed inside me, it didn't hurt as much. I winced and gasped as I stretched, but it was tolerable. Daddy's tongue and fingers caressing me helped take my mind off the pain.

"See, you're such a good girl, taking every inch of Daddy's cock. Now, can you move up and down for Daddy?"

I nodded and slowly did so. Up and down, over and over, all while he touched and kissed and licked me. Yes, yes, yes!

My Daddy continued to whisper how good I was doing and what a perfect little pussy I had.

"I knew you'd be able to take all of me. Your pussy is so soaked. You didn't want him. You wanted me, didn't you?"

I nodded and ground my hips against him.

"Say it. Say you want me more than him."

"I want you more than him."

He pulled back.

"I want you, Daddy," I groaned. "I don't want Milton. I want my Daddy forever and ever."

"What do you want exactly, Eleanor?"

"I want you to kiss me, touch me, and—"

"And what? Do you want me to fuck you?"

"Yes!"

"Then say it." He growled.

"I want you to fuck me!" I screamed as my body erupted. Warmth flooded my veins as Daddy continued to thrust into me, calling me his good girl and holding me to him.

My mouth collided with his. He pushed his tongue in and swirled around mine. I continued to move my hips the way he'd taught me until finally he stiffened and let out a groan. Something warm gushed into me, and he pulled out, satisfied. It wasn't until we came down that I realized I'd never actually asked where Milton was.

Rule Eleven - Callahan
Let her sleep.

"We need to go." The swan boat returned to its original position, having circled the path over and over while Eleanor and I rode the waves of passion and lust. She'd already redressed herself and was staring at me bashfully. I gave her a nod. While it had been great sex, it wasn't my finest hour.

I'd broken the code.

"I have so many questions," she said as I helped her out of the boat. She was barefoot and limping. I turned the power off, then scooped her into my arms and began the trek back to my motorcycle. She gave me a questioning look, and I smiled.

"A Daddy takes care of his Young Lady."

She relaxed into my arms, and I picked up the pace.

"How can you survive without a mask?" she asked after a while.

I swallowed. Did I dare tell her my secret?

"A few years ago, I discovered a bottle of pills. It's the same ones they give Young Ladies but for men. It's still in testing, but the papers I found with it said it would enable us to breathe above. So, I took them."

"And you didn't get caught?"

"Not yet. Once I figured out where to get more, I've been taking them ever since. This is the first time I've tried them out."

"And no one knew about it?"

Only Milton.

"No. And no one will." We reached the tram stairs. "I have to go retrieve my mask. Stay here." I set her down carefully and sprinted up the rickety metal stairs, collecting my mask and running back down. I was breathing heavily by the time I landed back on the ground, but Eleanor was safe. I slipped on my mask and picked her back up. "Let's get back to the bunker."

Our entrance was quiet. We managed to return to our rooms without anyone noticing, and in the morning, we acted as if nothing had happened. She was still an untouched Young Lady, and I was her bastard, bully Daddy. It killed me to think about what I'd done to her. If anyone found out, she'd be tossed to the elements, right along with me.

The next few days, we stayed quiet around each other. She didn't argue with me in public, and our first official mission to the above was done with very little fanfare. She did her job, I did mine, and we returned safe, sound, and miserable.

Every night, despite my twelve years of training, I fought the urge to go to her. I sat in my room, remembering the feel of her wet, velvety walls hugging my rigid cock, and how good it was to see her unravel around it. I wanted to do it again and again, but knowing I couldn't, I took care of myself, each time imagining her face in that moment of ecstasy.

I was going mad, and it appeared that so was she. Every morning, she complained of having trouble sleeping. I wanted to ask if it was because of me, but she didn't seem interested. I took her to the medic and then escorted her to her room.

While she was in the shower, I looked around again.

Perhaps there was a sign, something to tell me what was keeping her up at night. I rifled through her drawers and found a notebook with her name on it in cursive. Her diary.

My stomach tightened as I went to the last few pages and read her words. They were about me. She had kept it vague, not revealing what we'd done, but she had written that every night, she replayed it in her head and wanted more, but knowing she couldn't was killing her. She didn't want to be a Young Lady anymore.

The shower stopped, and I shoved the diary back and fled. I waited until I knew she'd taken the sleeping pills and was in bed before returning to her room.

Eleanor was in a deep sleep on her back. I pulled out her diary again and read through it in full. Each page was filled with dreams of something more than this life, and a strong desire to run away and never return. And the last week's entries were all about how she felt for me, and wanted to kiss and touch and, to quote her, 'do things Young Ladies were not allowed to even think about'. Once I finished, I set it back and stared at the bed. I wanted that too.

With my heart hammering in my chest, I crept to the bed.

God, she was beautiful. I could see her frame under the blanket, and my cock rose to attention. The memory of what she looked like bare was always prominent in my mind. Daring to be brave, I walked to the front of the bed and tugged on her blanket, bringing it down.

My heart dropped to my stomach as I gazed down upon her beautiful tan body. Her nightgown was short and barely covered her pink panties. I exposed her completely, tossing the blanket on the floor, and still, she didn't budge. My hands reached for her feet, running them up her smooth legs. As I slid up, I crawled onto the bed, spreading her legs wide as I moved between them.

My mouth watered as I leaned in at the apex of her thighs

and inhaled deeply. She smelled heavenly. I wanted a taste. Still nervous she'd wake, I ran my tongue along the front of her panties and down. Oh, what a tease. This wasn't enough. I needed to know exactly what her juices tasted like. What her silky pussy felt like against my tongue. Could she come while fast asleep?

I reached for her hips and dragged her panties down. She sighed, but her legs were deadweight as I lifted them and removed her underwear. My hands drifted along her slit, teasing it by poking in and out just a bit. Her body responded, despite the heavy slumber, slowly growing wet with arousal.

I stretched and reached for her breasts under her nightgown. She had no bra, and I pinched her nipples softly, eliciting a groan from her sleepy lips. I moved my head closer and parted her swollen pussy lips. I ran my tongue down her, taking in just how soaked she was. She tasted musky and lovely at the same time. Greedily, I wanted more. I lapped at her juices, sucked on her clit, and slid a finger into her entrance, fucking her with it.

Eleanor began to respond through the sedative sleepy haze. She moaned and bucked her hips. I held her firm and continued to ravish her clit and pussy like it was my last meal. It very well could be, if I were caught. But that made it even more fun. Tomorrow, she'd wake up, not knowing I was even here. But I'd be here every night. Bringing ourselves to orgasms.

My cock wept and strained as I ate her out. I stroked myself as I continued to suck and swirl around her clit. I'd never tasted pussy this good, and I wanted more and more of it. It was an aphrodisiac for all of my senses.

She wasn't just my Young Lady. She was my everything. She was mine.

I pushed lightly on her belly, and a sharp cry came from her as it did the trick. Her pussy suddenly began to pulse and grow even wetter, and I lapped up every single drop as she came all over my face. My cock pleaded for me to do something. I jerked myself over her pussy.

I lifted her gown to expose her breasts to me. I wanted to cover them in my cum. I moved closer, fingering her pussy again. She began to breathe faster, and I could feel my orgasm rising to the surface. I reached for her chin, tugging it open, just slightly, and then I exploded.

One, two, three spurts of cum landed on her lips, her breasts, and drizzled onto her belly. I stared at her lips in awe as I came. My salty fluid was so close to her tongue, I needed her to taste it.

I traced the cum, smearing it over her skin. I pushed my cum into her mouth and reflexively her tongue came out, and she swallowed. I dropped off the bed, put the blanket back on, and kissed her forehead.

She took it all so well.

And she was going to take it every night from now on.

Rule Twelve - Callahan
They are always watching.

"Attention!" The Young Ladies were settling in to watch a movie in the recreation room when they were interrupted by a red-faced warden. "Milton was found this morning. Impaled on metal poles on top of the tram ride at that Risky Rush Park you all love so much."

Gasps rang out. It took everything in me not to show my nerves. I glanced at the other Daddies and matched their shocked expressions. It had been nearly a month since I'd confronted Milton. I knew I should have gone back and taken his body down. I'd been too busy fucking his girl every night while she slept to bother.

"It looks like he was murdered, and we have reason to believe someone here knows something."

"When?" Eleanor stood up. Tears streamed down her face. "When did he die?"

"Weeks ago, his body was very rotted."

I flinched. Fuck, fuck fuck.

She let out a sharp squeak.

"Eleanor, do you know something?" the warden asked her. She shook her head vehemently.

"No, sir. I'm just upset. I'd like to go." She ran out of the room, and I had no choice but to follow her.

"Eleanor!" I stretched my arm out and sprinted after her.

"Leave me alone!" she cried and darted down a different hall. She tried to lose me, taking lefts and rights, but I was trained to keep my eye on her at all times, and eventually caught her, spinning her around. I squeezed her shoulders.

"Eleanor, please," I pleaded. "Let me explain."

"It was you. You killed him," she snapped. "Why? What did he ever do to you?"

"Milton, along with your original Daddy and some other Daddies, had planned to kidnap and rape you that night. They were going to kill you when they were done. I caught them discussing it and..."

Her eyes widened. "It was you. You killed my Daddy." She pulled away from me and backed into the wall. "You killed him and then took his place."

I put my hands up in innocence. "Yes, but not on purpose. I didn't want to take his place. I just wanted to save you."

"You're lying." She shook her head. "My Daddy would never."

"He would. Every generation has a Young Lady they choose, and this group had chosen you."

"That makes no sense." Tears poured from her eyes. "Why?"

"I can't answer that," I said truthfully. I had never heard of this ritual until I'd caught them in the act. It was vile, and I'd acted quickly.

"Eleanor!" The warden's voice boomed from a different hall and found us a moment later. He smiled tightly at us. I recognized the look. He wasn't happy. "We'd like to talk to you. About Milton."

"Why?" Her eyes flicked to me. "I told you I don't know anything."

"Yes, you did say that. I'd like to dive a little deeper. Come. You too, Callahan, she needs an escort."

I tried to follow her into the office, but he put his hand on my chest. "You stay here."

I nodded grimly. An hour later, Eleanor was released.

"I'm going to go to bed. It's been a long night," she said blankly. I led her back to our quarters. The moment the door slid shut, she perked her head up. "They think I did it."

"What? Why?" I hurried to her, embracing her tightly. "No. You couldn't have."

She sniffled. "I know. I told them that, but they kept telling me their story, trying to get me to agree to it. They said I went out to find Milton, he attacked me, and then I pushed him. They want me to go to the medic."

"What for?"

"T-they want to check if I'm a virgin."

It was as if they'd doused me with cold water. "Why? Did you tell them we—"

"No! Of course not. They found my underwear on the tram. And my shoes with my name in them. They think he raped me and that's why I killed him."

"But why does it matter?"

"They want to know if I'm pregnant."

That was it. They wanted Milton's genes to live on, and they wanted Eleanor to be carrying it. They wouldn't find his DNA, if they looked. *They'd find mine.*

"I don't know what to do," Eleanor confessed. "They'll kill us both."

I squeezed her hand. "We need to leave. Hurry, pack a bag, get your medicine, all of it. I'll do the same."

"Where are we going?" she cried out.

"Where else? We'll have to go above."

Bags slung over our shoulders, we waited. The warden was going to wait until morning. I knew his tactics too well. He was currently in his office or private quarters, planning it all. Ten Daddies, all armed, ready to shoot us the moment they discovered Eleanor wasn't carrying Milton's child.

I doubted she was even carrying mine, but it wouldn't matter. The moment they realized she wasn't producing an heir for the warden or Milton, she was useless. She'd been defiled, and that didn't make for a good Young Lady.

We waited until the middle of the night and quietly left her room. Eleanor had put on the dress she'd worn for her birthday.

"It's my most cherished item," she'd explained sadly.

There was only one way out of the bunker, and they could be waiting for us in that room. Much to my relief, we were alone. I took a PARA suit, a gas mask, and a gun. Then, we went up.

"He said that?" she asked as we climbed the ladder. "That he was going to do that to me?"

"He did. They normally didn't invite DITs to join but considering his status and his relationship with you, they decided to include him."

"Status?"

"He's the warden's son," I explained. "That's the only reason this is such a big deal. If it had been me, they wouldn't have cared if I was dead."

She grew quiet. It was true. People went missing all the time. It was a part of the job. But never had there been such a long search for them after. Everyone knew that once you stayed long enough above, you either became a creepie or a crawlie. Or, if you were lucky, you'd just die.

"You saw him. That day at the tram. What did he say?" We reached the ground and began our trek to the vehicles. I didn't want to tell her the truth. Despite all that I had told her, I knew she didn't want to believe it. She didn't want to face the fact that the man she'd crushed on for years was a predator.

"He lured you out to finish the job. Milton was in the mid-stages of turning into a creepie. He took his mask off and told me to do the same, hoping I'd start the change too. And when I didn't, he turned on me. It was either him or I, and if I died, then when you got up to the platform, he would have killed you too."

Clouds thundered above us, and I looked up. The sky was dark, even more than usual for nighttime. A bright light flashed in the sky, and then slow, small drips of rain began to fall from the sky. Oh no, acid rain. I reached for her and looked for the nearest roof to shield us.

"Ouch!" Eleanor squeaked. I reached for the arm she was holding and examined it. Where the rain had touched her, a small red mark remained. Only a small red mark. She was immune.

"Ouch! The rain is pinching me!"

"It's acid rain. Don't let it get in your mouth or eyes."

I hurried her along and then stopped in my tracks when we reached the gates and found the lot empty. Completely empty.

"Nice try, Daddy."

We spun around to see the warden and all the other Daddies. They'd followed us out here. Or, maybe they'd been out here before us and had been waiting. I shoved Eleanor behind me.

"Just let us go," I said. "Just let us leave, and there'll be no trouble."

"No trouble?" The warden stepped forward and laughed. I pulled my gun over my shoulder, and in sync, all the others did the same, aiming their weapons at me. "You see, soldier," the warden said, "it's too late. We know how it went down. Milton had a camera on his person. You're already in trouble."

Rule Thirteen - Callahan
Trust is a powerful thing.

I didn't believe him. We'd never had cameras on our missions, let alone a birthday party. Where would Milton have gotten one? The warden was bluffing. He wanted me to confess.

"I have no idea what you're talking about," I said.

"You were the last one to see Milton alive, weren't you?" He stepped forward, his boots crunching on the damp soil. Our masks were sizzling from the acid rain. It was steadily picking up speed.

"I don't know. It was chaos."

He pointed his gun at me. "Was it? Because it appears that only two people left the bunker the night Milton was impaled on those spikes."

I pushed Eleanor back, all the while looking for an exit. There wasn't one. It was either the bunker or—I blinked. Behind the line of Daddies was a four-wheeler. That would get us far enough to find help, shelter, something.

"I didn't have anything to do with that," I lied.

"Your fellow DITs told us everything. They saw you attack Eleanor's Daddy and then turn on Milton, but we weren't sure why. We came up with a plan, and you told on yourself every step of the way."

They'd assigned me to Eleanor on purpose. They wanted me to break my oaths. They wanted to catch me telling on myself, and they'd succeeded. I shook my head, but I knew it was pointless. "You don't have proof."

"Oh yes, we do. Give us the girl," he snarled. "Give back the Young Lady, and we'll remove your gear and leave you here without another word. Fight us, and you'll regret it."

I felt small hands on my hips. Eleanor clutched me, squeezing me tight.

"I'm not letting you take her. She deserves to live a life, free of your rules."

"Rules she agreed to," he argued. The more he spoke, the more his mask began to fog. All of our gas masks were beginning to fog.

"She was eight!" I roared, embracing her. Then I looked at the warden. "An eight-year-old child can't decide her entire life. I'm not letting her go. I love her."

"Love?" he laughed, joined in by the Daddies. "Love isn't real. You're speaking with your cock, son. Give her back, and I'm sure when you're a creepie, you can find some bar to get crawlie pussy or something. She's not special."

"Then why do you want her so badly?"

Eleanor hugged me, her body trembling. I wasn't sure if it was from fear or the rain. Her skin was still completely unscathed, despite the ground sizzling under our feet. "Just find another little girl to take her place."

The warden let out a growl and lunged for her. I pushed her back and collided with the older man, shoving him back. His gun fell out of his hands but he didn't go for it. Instead, he tackled me to the ground and reached for my helmet.

"We'll handle it now. Save a bullet." He unclipped my mask and tore it off my head before I could stop him. There was a moment of silence as everyone waited for me to start gasping for air. But I didn't. The rain hit my face, and I winced at the wetness, but not at the poison it held. It was a sharp pinch if that. I was immune too. The pills did work.

"What the—Why aren't you dying?" he demanded. I shoved him off me and stood. All the Daddies stared at me in shock as the rain continued to pelt me. I took off my gloves and PARA suit jacket, stripping down to just my pants. Acid rain poured onto my exposed body, and still, I lived.

"We've been lied to!" I announced. "The Young Ladies aren't the only ones immune. All of us who have been assigned and turned into Daddies can survive above without suits and masks."

"Why haven't they told us?" one of the Daddies asked.

"Because how else would they keep us in line? They need us to be afraid, or their whole system collapses. See for yourself!"

The warden scurried over to the line. He wasn't so sure either. They stared at me in abject horror as I became soaked and still unharmed. They spoke amongst themselves and finally took off their masks and tossed them onto the ground.

Bingo.

An instant later, the rain hit their skin and burned holes into them. They screamed as their faces began to melt and their lungs filled with poisonous chemicals. They dropped to the ground and jerked until one by one, they died.

I turned to Eleanor, who was staring in horror at the scene. I took her in my arms and for the first time, unashamedly, I leaned down and pressed my lips to hers. .

"You love me?" she asked.

"I do. Always have. Just... never realized that's what it was."

Eleanor ran her hand over my bare chest and kissed me again. Our lips parted and our tongues danced in the madness of the moment. Her hands explored my body, and mine soon found her breasts, running my thumbs across her protruding nipple. She groaned, and my body responded in kind.

"I-I can't take it anymore." She tugged on my pants, unbuckling them. "It's all I can think about. Every night, I dream of being with you again. Of having you inside me. I need you now."

"Now?" I glanced over at the bodies. Some were still twitching. Their skin hung off, their eyes melted, their bone exposed. She looked too and then nodded.

"Now. I don't care. Take me, Daddy."

I led her to our escape vehicle and ushered her onto my lap. Pulling out my cock, she pushed up her white dress and slid her panties to the side. In a moment, our bodies were colliding in glorious ecstasy. It was pleasure and pain from the stinging rain that held me to her. It was our own personal punishment for what we'd done to get here, but it was worth every drop of rain that hit our skins.

She ground against me, pleading for me to make her come. I tugged down the dress, licking and sucking her breasts, thrusting into her, demanding her to do the same for me. We were panting and wincing and screaming and crying until finally she threw her head back and clenched her pussy tight around my needy cock. Her orgasm triggered my own, and it was magnificent.

We stared at each other for a long moment after, steadying our breaths and resting our foreheads together. Finally, I leaned back and took the helmet out of the passenger's seat and handed it to her.

"Put this on and get behind me."

She slid off, adjusted her dress, and straddled me from behind.

"Yes, Daddy."

"Good girl," I muttered. I glanced one last time at the pile of bodies. We could never go back. The warden wasn't top dog. There would be people looking for him, and once they found the massacre, they'd come for us. "Now, hold me tight. It's gonna be a long ride."

"Where are we going?" She leaned against me, wrapping her arms tightly around my middle.

I knew there was only one answer. She'd have a lot of questions, which I'd answer on the way. I turned on the machine and revved the engine. We were going somewhere no one knew about Young Ladies, Daddies or what we'd done. Somewhere we could be free.

"We're going to go find another bunker."

The End

One last thing before you leave the theater

Thank you for reading Like Father Like Slaughter. If you enjoyed it, please consider leaving a rating or review. Reviews are extremely important to authors and helps us continue to create books.

Fun fact about my Final Girls Featurettes series: If a specific story gets popular enough, I'll turn it into a full length novel.

Even Funner fact: This novella got so popular, I have made the decision to turn it into a full length version, titled 'Hips, Lips, Apocalypse.

Preorder it here:
Hips, Lips, Apocalypse

About the Author

After watching *Heathers* and listening to My Chemical Romance one too many times in her teens, Chicana author, Tylor Paige, was drawn to the darkness where the villains were still villains, but deserved love stories too.

Shifting her focus to Horror Romance, Tylor writes snarky, psycho vampires, troubled but beautiful Goblin Kings, and slashers so sexy you'll be begging your partner to buy a mask.

When she's not writing about women railing the villains, she enjoys watching horror films, sewing, comic books, and participating in her local community theatre. At the time of this update Tylor has now written and published twelve full length novels and one novella.

Oh, and feel free to call her Ty. She prefers it.

Also by Tylor Paige

Final Girl Series:

Slash or Pass

Slay Less

Knife, Comment, Share

Hips, Lips, Apocalypse

Final Girls 5

Final Girl Featurettes: (100 page novellas!)

Like Father Like Slaughter

Little Deaths: a Vampire Mafia series

Seven Little Deaths

Lay Your Body Down

Bury Me in Blood

Little Taste of Death (FREE VALENTINES SHORT!)

Standalones:

Surrender to Forever- a Goblin King reimagining

Find me all over

Www.Tylorpaige.com
  https://linktr.ee/Tylorpaige
  Facebook.com/Tylorpaigeauthor
  Instagram: @Tylorpaige
  TikTok: @authortylorpaige
  Join the Tylor Paige's Whorror Babies group on Facebook!
  https://www.facebook.com/groups/376190999768893/?ref=share